Skies of Blue

Pamela Ackerson

WHAT A WONDERFUL WORLD

Pamela Ackerson

Books by Pamela Ackerson

The Cedar Ridge Hills Museum Time Travel Series

The House on Cedar Ridge
Locke Manor—Coming in October 2022
Cedar Ridge Hills Museum—Coming in March 2023

Skies of Blue ~ Originally from the Late to Love Charity
Anthology

The Wilderness Time Travel Series

Across the Wilderness
Into the Wilderness
Wilderness Bound
Warriors of the Wilderness
Out of the Wilderness
The Wilderness Series E-book Box Set

PI Series Time Travel

Garrett's Ghost
The Gingerbread House
Living the Wright Life
PI Time Travel E-book Box Set

Historical Fiction

Dear Margaret,

Nonfiction

I Was Just a Radioman (A memoir of a Pearl Harbor
survivor, Black Cat, and decorated veteran.)
The Prequel to Be More Successful with Marketing and
AdvertiZing
Be More Successful with Marketing and AdvertiZING
I am a Runner — the Memoirs of a Sepsis Survivor
Simple Herbal Recipes: Return to the Olde Ways

A Granny Pants Story   (Children's Stories)

The Long and Little Doggie
Riley Gets into Predicaments
Available in Spanish:
El Perrito Largo y el Perrito Pequeno (La Serie del Perrito
Largo y Pequeno)

Short Stories

The Clere's Restaurant Short Story Collection

Sunday at 7
With a Side of Love
Winds from the Past
The Throuple with Love
The Best Catch of His Life
Clere's Restaurant Collection Box Set

A Rosa for Russell ~ Historical Fiction Short Story

Pambling Roads Journals —

Pages for you to fill in the blanks! Nurture your creativity with Pambling Roads State Journals, interactive journals designed to spark imagination and self-motivation. They include historical trivia and tidbits about each state, and a small section by the author sharing her travels.

States:
Alabama   Arizona   Arkansas   California   Colorado
Florida   Georgia   Idaho   Illinois   Indiana   Iowa
Kansas   Kentucky   Louisiana   Maine   Maryland
Massachusetts   Michigan   Minnesota   Mississippi
Missouri   Montana   Nebraska   Nevada   New
Hampshire   New Mexico   New York   North Dakota
Oregon   Rhode Island   South Carolina   South Dakota
Ohio   Oklahoma   Tennessee   Texas   Utah   Vermont
Virginia   Washington   Wisconsin   Washington, D.C.
Wyoming

Fortune Cookie Wisdom Journal

*Almost all of the paperback books are available in Large Print

Skies of Blue

Pamela Ackerson

Editing: WordRefiner.com
Cover Design: BetiBub

PamelaAckerson.net
@PamAckerson

Chapter One

Janet Nelson parked her vehicle on the slight incline near the entrance of Cedar Ridge Hills Museum. She turned the car off only to hear it continue to run before it coughed, chugged, burped, and made other colorful bodily function noises before it stopped with a sigh of relief.

The door made a piercing screech, objecting her to exit from the car. It continued its complaining until she slammed it shut.

You're never going to make it...

She ignored the condescending voice and took a deep, cleansing breath.

The majestic manor sat on the crest of the hill. Seen from the cliffs and Lake Superior, it shared the summer sky. A faint ray of light appeared on the far horizon dispelling the darkness. The morning breeze cleared the dawn mist shrouding the distant boundary dividing heaven and earth.

It hinted at the secrets and mysteries within the haunted walls of the museum until they dissolved into each other. The ancient cliffs projected upwards, a hundred feet from the lake below.

Janet inhaled the comforting fresh air. The lake beyond the rock face was calm and motionless. The curling waves were gentle. The lake was never still, the massive expanse of Superior beckoned, pulling the tides to a distant shore. The unseen currents demanded obedience. The force of the great lake forever called the people of Locke Bay to its shores.

The museum was a vast and sprawling place. Its rooms were many, and its halls elaborate. It stretched from high towers to deep cellars.

Of all its many rooms, there was one built deep into the very foundation of its secrets. One room roused different emotions in different people; the 'campfire' rituals inspired stories revealing its secrets of transcendental travel. To others, it was simple curiosity.

To a handful, it was fear and desperation.

The great walls of Locke Manor weathered years of troubles and happiness.

Janet used to play manhunt among the deserted hallways, partying with her friends before the state's purchase. The college students considered it an initiation of sorts, a rite of passage…to spend one night in the sanatorium section among the haunted halls of Locke Manor.

The warmth and radiance of the sun shining down on the great house couldn't remove the woeful shadows clouding her days. They haunted her, just as the halls of the great manor were haunted by its past.

Somehow, all those wide-eyed, naïve dreams came crashing down around her. Janet was born with a silver spoon in her mouth, and life served on a silver platter. However, no one could accuse her of being lazy. She was raised to work for what she wanted. Her parents were financially comfortable, not her. She had to make her own way.

Entitled was a dirty word in her family.

She'd married into a more affluent family, new money. Of course, it wasn't unexpected. However, somewhere along the line, she'd lost the silver spoon, and dropped the silver platter until it shattered and broke into tiny little pieces.

She literally ran away from the comforts of wealth; and began her new life with a quarter in her pocket.

For her, it was the last straw. Lines became more important to him than the roof over their heads. He'd lost his temper when he found out she threw it in the trash. She touched her tongue to the tooth he broke.

She fell against the door and grabbed the closest thing. Janet had thrown the large formal lamp at him. When he ducked, it gave her a chance to get away from him. She ran from the house before he had a chance to grab her again.

Janet had found a quarter on the ground while walking to her friend's house. She had nothing but the clothes on her back. She started her new life with absolutely nothing but that quarter.

She was forced into hiring a lawyer to pick up her and Aiden's belongings, the ones he hadn't destroyed.

Everything went up in smoke. Like the phoenix, her life was reborn.

She lost her job and dropped out of college. So much for her master's degree.

You'll never make it without me, princess.

Yeah, watch me.

She may have a broken-down car, a tiny apartment she shared with two other people, and was working in a small diner…but she'd be damned if she would go crawling back to him.

She even started dating a year ago. It was a freaking disaster, a huge mistake. Her divorce was pending. Even though there hadn't been any physical relationship, X accused her of adultery. She hadn't found a job to support herself, let alone their son.

When X refused to return Aiden on one of his visitation weekends, all hell broke loose.

She retained a small apartment with roommates. He had a large home, a bank account, possession of the vehicles, and an expensive lawyer. He'd accused her of doing all the things he'd done to her.

The X used it all against her.

You want your son back? Then come home and be a real wife.

Her divorce was finalized last month. He promised he would break her. He almost did. She'd lost the only thing that mattered, custody of her son. Shared parental responsibility, Janet had him 50% of the time, but Aiden lived with X.

He bragged about how he'd bought her lawyer.

Despair threatened her heart.

Two years passed since she walked away from a life of luxury, and she still had the quarter. It was a reminder that tomorrow was a promise of hope and second chances.

She stared at the door to the museum.

This job could be her redemption, a new beginning to change not only her life, but also the lives of others around her.

Janet knew what it was to live in darkness, to find a moment of reprieve, only to be plunged into obscurity again. She understood the undercurrents hidden behind superficial smiles.

When she'd first come to Locke Bay, Cedar Ridge Hills lured her to it. She was fascinated by the imposing manor house. It separated the boundaries of the mystery from the truth and the boundaries within the mind.

Janet took a deep breath before entering the Cedar Ridge Hills Museum. Her hands shook. She had no qualifications, no inkling of what she was getting into, nor did she have any idea of how much she should be asking for a wage.

All she knew was what George told her.

Sweet and wonderful George Greene was one of the docents at the museum. He'd chatted with her when business was slow at the diner, and they'd gotten to know each other. They'd been looking for a new tour guide, and according to George, she'd be perfect for the position.

"Good morning."

"Good morning, George. I wasn't expecting you to be here."

"Me either, but it appears our newest curator has exited the building."

Her mouth dropped. "Another one? Three in the last month?"

He grunted. "Four."

She frowned, disappointed. She hadn't realized how much she hoped to get the position.

He locked the door behind her. "Come on. Let's have some coffee."

Following him, she rubbernecked her way down the hall toward the kitchen area.

"Don't fret. Since I'm the one doing the hiring today, you have the job."

"Really?"

"It's all yours."

"I'll need to give in two-week notice. But I can work part-time until then."

"Absolutely. We can start your training today if you'd like."

Janet laughed. "I like. I like."

Chapter Two

Fifteen minutes before the tour started, her phone rang. "Hey, what happened? I called last night and left a message."

"Yeah, I heard it. If you don't pick Aiden up at five like you're supposed to, you're not getting him."

"I can't leave. It's why I called you last night. I'm the only one scheduled to be here for the tour. I can be there a few minutes after six."

"Why don't you get a real job?"

"This is a *real* job."

X snorted, "Minimum wage is less than what you were making in tips at the dive."

"It wasn't a dive. And, I'm making more than minimum wage. I can't just leave."

"Then don't bother coming to get him, princess. This is the decision you made when you left me."

The phone clicked. X hung up on her.

She stared at the phone. A lump formed in her throat. She didn't get Aiden on her last weekend because his parents were in town. She understood. His parents wanted to spend time with their grandson. She gave up her weekend for them.

Now, she can't get him again. A few hours every Wednesday wasn't enough. She'd have to give her notice. This won't do.

Distracted, she moved through the tour trying to figure out if he'd let her get Aiden if she showed up an hour late.

A patrol car sat in front of his house. The officer got out of the car when she arrived.

Her car clunked, sputtered, and screeched before it grunted in relief. Janet could feel the heat of humiliation turning her face red. Her heart clenched.

"Are you Janet Flanagan Nelson?"

The lump in her throat made it hard to answer. "Yes."

"We've been asked to remove you from the property."

Her heart raced. "I'm here to pick up my son. It's my weekend."

"According to the paperwork, if you don't show up within a certain amount of time to get your son…"

"I'm here now. I was at work. I called him, twice!"

"I'm sorry. My hands are tied. You'll have to take it up in the courts, ma'am."

She left. Her eyes flooded with tears. She pulled over when she got near the park.

Janet couldn't hold back the soul-wrenching sobs.

When will this stop? Please make it stop!

What had she done? She should've gone back to him as everyone advised. She never told them why they split. She explained they no longer got along and had grown apart. He told them she'd been having a mid-life crisis.

Ten years of marriage down the drain because she was selfish, and couldn't take anymore. What was wrong with her?

She gritted her teeth. Stupid, stupid, stupid. She should've stayed and just taken it. What were a few bruises and backhands? She could've stayed out of the way, avoided the black eyes, dark bruises on her hands and legs.

The problem was Janet could see it coming, and she refused to cower or back down. The warnings were in his eyes — the fierce anger, and the demonic death stare.

Their manor was her sanctuary and her prison.

Her phone dinged. *If you had stayed with me, you'd have a nice life and your son. When you said you'd never come back to me, I promised I'd break you. I know the only thing that matters to you is Aiden, and now he's mine.*

Defiance gave her strength. She would *not* let him break her.

The next morning, she knew her battle plan. George was sitting in the kitchen area scouring through some old paperwork.

He chimed, "Good morning."

"Morning." She looked at the papers. "Looking for anything in particular?"

"Yes, my long-lost brother."

"Brother?"

"We both stayed here at the foundling home before we were adopted out. I haven't been able to find him. With more access on the internet, I was hoping it'd be easier. So far no luck."

"I'm guessing the adoptive parents changed your names?"

He nodded, absorbed in his search. "They kept my first and middle names, George Albert. I just hope the papers weren't lost or destroyed. These locked adoptions are impossible to penetrate. Unless the other siblings are looking too."

"I'm sure your brother is looking also. But, if he isn't computer literate, he may not know there are websites where posts are made searching for adopted relatives."

"There are websites?"

"Yes. How were you looking?"

"I was just Googling his name."

She opened the box on the chair and grabbed the new pamphlets. "Do a search on 'how to find my brother'. Have you tried finding him through your parents' real names?"

George sighed, and shook his head. "I didn't even think of that."

She plopped down in her seat. "Change of subject, please. I have a question."

"Shoot."

"Can we change the last tour to begin at three so I can be out of here by five o'clock? At least on Fridays?"

He frowned. "Is there a problem?"

Janet winced. "Sort of. I need to pick up my son at five on Fridays."

"No worries, we'll work something out. If Patti can't do it, then I will."

She kissed his cheek. "You're the best."

"Don't say that just yet, I have a favor."

"Anything."

"Can you stay here until I find a curator? One who stays more than a few days anyway. We can't keep leaving the museum and grounds unattended during all of this renovating."

Her finger pointed downward. "Here?"

He wanted her to stay at the museum. With all the haunted spirits, and specters, etc.?

George nodded. "And maybe take over some of the curator's work?"

She sucked in a quick breath. "Of course. As long as there's no problem with Aiden staying too?"

"Do you think he'd want to do anything else?"

There was a knock on the door, before a man entered. She'd never seen him before. It was obvious by his clothing he was one of the construction workers.

"Good morning, Teri."

"Morning, Mr. Greene."

"This is Janet. She's one of our tour guides. Janet, this is Teri Olson. He's the foreman with the electric company who will be doing the rewiring in the east wing."

Teri put his hand out.

She diverted her eyes downward and took the offered greeting. "How do you do?"

"Good. Looking forward to working here." He looked around. "I've always been fascinated by this place."

Janet smiled. "That makes three of us."

"Thanks for coming in on a Saturday." George waved Teri toward the office. "Let's take a look at what you got so far."

She watched them walk away. *Nice.*

He looked like he worked out at the gym. Gorgeous eyes, average looking, little bit of a beer belly, and definitely not her type. Nothing at all like X who was very good-looking, popular, and radiated prep-school attitude and education.

Perhaps she should consider dating someone who wasn't her type. She stretched her neck to watch Teri. There was something about him...

Her radar ears heard his subdued remark as the two men walked away. "She a bit shy?"

George responded, "I thought so, too, at first. And then I got to know her."

With the museum closed on Sundays, it gave Janet the opportunity to bring in some boxes, clothes, her computer, and a few necessities. She stuffed the car with her and Aiden's possessions.

The car gagged, sputtered, and passed out about ten feet from the parking spot. Poor thing, the excess weight was too much for the old clunker. She sighed when the driver's door screamed its objections. It continued screaming as it rocked back and forth while she made a sad attempt to push it forward.

She hadn't told her roommates anything except she'd be gone for a few days. Janet wasn't about to give up her room. It'd be worth continuing to pay the fifty a week. Who knew how long it'd take to find a curator who stayed.

She could use the extra two hundred for so many things. Janet looked at the sky. To think, a few years ago she hadn't thought twice about spending that much on a wallet.

She grabbed a box.

You're useless.

Get out of my head. You won't break me.

You're never going to make it without me.

It isn't the gold in your pocket, X. It's the gold in your heart that counts.

She'd been on the phone with Aiden for over an hour the night before. He was thrilled when she'd told him they'd be staying there.

Yeah, she was too. Just what she wanted, to stay in a freaking haunted castle.

The sarcasm rang false even in her own ears. She *loved* the idea of staying in the haunted manor for an undisclosed amount of time. It was an opportunity of a lifetime.

When she told X, he'd responded with his usual disdain. Your new coworkers must think you're pathetic; they had to offer you a free stay in the haunted monstrosity. At least you won't have to drive the moving junkyard to work.

George told her to tell her roommates she was moving out. Janet just couldn't. Not yet. She needed the safety net, a backup plan.

The last two years of her marriage, she kept stashing money. She knew she wanted out, but it was mainly to pay the bills.

If there was money in the bank, he had to spend it. It burned a hole in his pocket. He had to have all the games, all the latest toys, and the best of the best when he went glamping.

They'd sold their house when he transferred.

He couldn't find another house he liked. Then, they couldn't agree on what to buy. By the time they found something, he'd spent the down-payment money.

He found out about the savings account and spent it. X knew she'd hide backup/safety money for the 'rainy days'. He'd found it, too.

The two of them made more than enough to be comfortable. However, for the last few years they were always struggling.

Then she found them. The empty baggies. It all started making sense.

His temper, his drinking…

When she confronted him, again, he blew up. It was the worst he'd ever been. That was the day she ran, and never went back.

He'd already had a ferociously hot temper to start with, but over the years, it had gotten worse. Did she learn to keep her mouth shut? No, of course not. It would make sense not to poke the bear. Why would she listen to reason, and stay down? She'd get back up off the floor and stand up to him, fight back. Janet couldn't count the number of times they'd butted heads and she'd ended up flying across the room.

She took a deep breath. No more. She needn't worry anymore.

If it hadn't been for George suggesting she apply for a job at the museum, she'd still be slinging waffles at the diner.

Chapter Three

Over the next few months, she'd finally told her roommates she'd be permanently moving out. George and Jacob, the groundskeeper, taught her how to use tools, work on the car, repair drywall, and lay ceramic tile. Teri, the electrician, even showed her how to change out an outlet. Simple, but she learned and it thrilled her.

Janet felt quite accomplished.

Even with all the haunted noises coming from the walls, Aiden loved staying at the manor. He even helped with some chores for the museum. X was his usual, *aren't you tired of being a charity case?*

When X caught her learning how to change her oil, he leaned in and quietly whispered, "Grease suits you. Perhaps you should become a grease monkey."

Aiden grabbed some tools and helped. X wasn't happy. He slammed the car door and took off in a huff.

It put a smile on her face. It shouldn't have, but it did.

George remarked, "Guess he doesn't like you becoming so self-sufficient."

Teri came around the corner, "What'd you do to piss him off this time?"

Aiden spoke from underneath the car, "Daddy says Mommy's been slumming for so long she's becoming ghetto fabulous."

Janet could feel the heat of anger flush her cheeks.

Teri winked. "Aw, he thinks you're fabulous in everything you do. So do I."

George chuckled.

Later that night Janet, Patti, and Jacob were at the Superior Oyster Bar and Grill when Teri and Kaitlyn entered.

After introductions, Teri excused himself and went up to the bar to order drinks. Janet had gone to the ladies room. Kaitlyn came in as she was washing her hands.

"Are you enjoying staying at Cedar Ridge Hills?"

"Yes, I like it. It's kind of cool staying in such a grand manor."

"Aren't you scared?"

Janet shrugged. "It's a great estate. Even with its many creaks settling in the night. Nothing to be afraid of."

Except when there were storms. They rattled the old manor and shook the windows. The cries of the dead shattered the hollows of the dark shadows and sent shivers up her spine.

Aiden loved it.

"You're a brave soul. They say the house stood deserted for so long because the living sought refuge in more peaceful settings. When the Locke family left, an evil spirit remained to roam the cold, empty corridors."

"My, you do have a vivid imagination." Janet started to leave.

"Are you interested in Teri?"

"I'm not interested in anyone at this point in my life." *Yes, I absolutely am. But, I'm not ready.*

"Well, just so you know. We've been together for a long time—over fifteen years. It's obvious to me you're interested; I can tell by the way you were looking at him. And if you hurt him, you'll have to deal with *me*."

"You're together? I thought he was dating Madison."

"Oh, that's over. Besides, we have an open marriage."

Married? Her heart frowned. Janet opened the door, and spoke quietly before leaving, "I'm not interested."

A few months later, Teri asked her out on a date. She'd gracefully turned him down. She didn't care if they had an 'open' marriage. It wasn't for her. Any interest she'd had toward him went out the window when Kaitlyn informed her they were married.

She suffered more than enough drama in her life with X. She certainly didn't need anymore. His wife gave her the distinct impression she thrived on creating chaos and drama.

Then Aiden, George, et al. started on her.

Teri's fun, Mom.

You're good for each other.

Give him a chance.

I understand you think you can't fall in love again…

It's never too late.

Almost a year after they'd met, Teri came into the kitchen and handed her a pot of geraniums. "Happy birthday."

Her favorite.

George grinned.

Janet could feel the rush of heat tickle her cheeks red. "Thank you. How'd you know?"

"Aiden." He poured himself a cup of coffee. "I'd like to take you to dinner, to celebrate."

She shook her head. "No, but thank you anyway."

His eyes darkened, and he stood. "Well, I need to get on with the inspection."

George frowned. "Why won't you give him a chance?"

She snapped, and headed to her office. "Really, George. This is freaking tiresome. What makes you think I'd want to even consider dating a married man?"

"Married! He isn't married."

Her chest clenched. "What?"

"What makes you think he's married?"

"His wife?"

He glowered. "He's not married."

"Kaitlyn told me they'd been together for fifteen years and had an open marriage. It's fine and dandy for other people. More power to them, it's just not for me."

"She's his *roommate*. Kaitlyn needed a place to stay after her divorce and he had a room. They're just friends."

She leaned against the doorframe. "Why would she lie?"

"Beats me." He leaned on his elbows, "Well, at least now I know why you wouldn't give him a chance."

A lump formed in Janet's throat. "I've got work to do."

She slammed the folder on her desk.

He isn't married. All this time, she'd pushed away her feelings and attraction toward him because she thought...

Why would Kaitlyn lie?

Her intercom buzzed.

Patti spoke, "X is on one."

"Thanks, Patti."

Janet chuckled. She even had the group calling him X. "Hello."

"Hey, you can't pick up Aiden today. I'm sending him to Texas for the summer."

Her heart thumped against her chest. "No, you're not. I have him for the first half of the summer and we're going to see my parents next week. They haven't seen him for months."

X snorted, "Too late. I put him on the plane this morning."

She growled, "You can't do that."

"I just did."

The silence was deafening. She stared at the phone, furious at X. He knew darn well by the time the lawyers got together and settled this, the summer would be over.

She clenched her teeth. Her right eye started doing a northern lights dance, warning a ferocious headache was pending. She'd never experienced such pain until her divorce. It scared her until the doctor told her it was a sign of a migraine.

Janet took several deep breaths to calm herself. It didn't help.

She called X back. "You can't do that."

"It's done. There's nothing you can do."

"You f—"

She swore at a dead phone line. She hit speed dial.

"Don't you *dare* hang up on me again. This is my time with him."

"He doesn't want to stay with you in the decrepit, haunted mausoleum. He told me he didn't want to spend his summer with you. He can't stand being there."

"That's bull!"

"No, it's not. He just didn't know how to tell you."

"Bullsh—"

"He doesn't want to be there with you. When will you get it through your thick skull? No one wants you. No one wants to be around you. The only time anyone wants to have anything to do with you is when no one else is available. You're the *backup*, honey. The backup daughter, the backup sister, and now I'm getting married, you'll be the backup mom. They all just tolerate you."

"That's not true." Her heart clenched. She could feel the tears filling her eyes.

"Yes, it is, and you know it."

He hung up.

No one wants you. They all just tolerate you.

Janet sat down and stared out the window. Tears poured from the corners of her eyes. She couldn't stop them. Jumping up she ran to the door and locked it.

She slid down onto the floor and broke down. Hard, sobbing muffled cries poured from her soul. The tears flowed, mourning the broken dreams, and the loss of hope.

Aiden. Why didn't he want to spend the summer with her? They'd talked about all the things they were going to do. He'd been so excited. What made him change his mind?

What did she do wrong?

Aiden, why?

Chapter Four

The old manor had been cantankerous the night before. It felt her anger, her frustration, and her failures. Janet felt distanced from the great house. A numbness filled her heart. She saw no pleasure in the sunlight, only the darkness of the emotional prison cell in which she was to die.

Aiden left for Texas. Was he frightened by the haunted manor? Did he truly not want to be with her?

Was X being honest in his implacable, ever so cold, and calculated way? Brutal honesty was his way. Did people tolerate her presence? Were they just being kind?

She blinked as the faint rays of sunlight crept across the side of the walls of the great house. The brilliant tuft of sunlight brightened the world of Cedar Ridge Hills. It chased away and mocked the wails echoing in the halls during the darkest of night.

All was silent except for the cries of the seagulls overhead. She opened the window and heard the buzz of the bees below in the red cluster bottlebrush tree.

Janet closed her eyes and faced the sun. *A new day, and the promise of tomorrow.*

Aiden will be back the first week of August.

How was she going to tell her parents?

She added a little more make-up to hide the dark circles, and headed downstairs.

As she walked down the hall, Janet smelled the fresh-brewed coffee.

"Good morning, you're here early."

George handed her a cup of coffee.

"I found some information about my brother. But, the surname of the adoptive parents was blackened out."

"Address?"

"Yes! I've already sent a letter. It's in the post box for the mailman to pick up."

"Awesome. Let's keep our fingers crossed."

"Did you have fun last night? Where's Aiden?"

"He's in Texas."

"When did he go to Texas?"

"Yesterday."

"On your birthday? I thought the two of you had plans last night to celebrate your birthday."

"He flew out yesterday morning."

"So, you were alone on your birthday…"

"It's   just   a   birthday, George."

"No, I know how much you like celebrating things like that. I wish I had known. We could've all met at the Grill."

Her eye starting ticking. "It's okay."

"Sounds to me like X did it on purpose."

I wouldn't put it past him. "Nah, he wouldn't." Janet shrugged. "Aiden wanted to go see his grandparents and the opportunity was there for him to go."

George frowned. "When will he be back?"

"The end of the summer."

28

"What about all your plans?"

She looked down. *Don't let him see how upset you are.* "He wanted to go."

"What about the car shopping the two of you were going to do today?"

"It'll wait."

He grunted and shook his head. "He was so excited about going with you to pick out a car."

She grimaced, "I guess he changed his mind."

"You going to wait until he gets back? You can keep using my car if you need to."

"No. I can put in a new transmission."

"Janet, for the three thousand dollars it's going to cost you to put in a new transmission and get the car running properly can put a nice down payment on a used vehicle."

"I know. After calling me unrealistically stubborn, my parents said the same thing."

"I understand why they want to help you, and I completely get why you don't want to take their money. I get it. Honest, I do."

"Can't say I haven't been tempted." She slathered her muffin with butter.

"Why don't we go looking this afternoon? I don't mind."

"I don't want to bother you."

"Nah, I like spending other people's money. Especially on big stuff like cars."

She laughed.

Later in the afternoon, George and Janet visited three dealerships.

"Let's call it a day."

George suggested, "We can look again on Saturday, if you'd like."

"Okay."

George turned down a side street to avoid traffic. A few minutes later, they both saw the car. It was in front of a house with a 'for sale' sign on it.

"This is nice."

"Nissan Sentra, good car," George added.

Janet was dialing the number on the car when someone came out of the house.

"Hello, may I help you?"

"Are you the owner? Can you tell us about the car?"

"Sure." He put his hand out, "Jeff."

"I'm George, and this is Janet."

Jeff unlocked the car, popped the hood, and started it for them. He and George inspected the engine.

Janet sat in the driver's seat, checking out the interior, dash, odometer, and radio. "Can we take it for a ride?"

"I can't leave right now. Wife isn't home to watch the kids."

George asked, "I can leave the keys to my car as collateral."

Jeff hesitated for a moment. "Sure."

"We'll only be gone for a few minutes."

"Okay."

The two drove off and parked at the museum. George continued to inspect the car. "Looks like a good deal."

"I was thinking about offering him twelve. Is it too low?"

"No, but fifteen is reasonable."

"I only qualify for ten, and the car's three years old."

"I can…"

"No." It came out harder than she intended. "Thank you, but I can't borrow money from you.

George nodded, "Okay, let's see if he'll bite."

"And if he'll take a check to hold it."

Jeff agreed to thirteen. Janet got all the information she needed for the bank and wrote him a check for $500. The two headed to the bank and finished the necessary paperwork.

No year had been longer for Janet since she'd left X that fateful day with nothing in her pocket. Buying the car gave her hope. Soon the struggles were over. The relief she felt was bliss. Waiting for her life to settle down to a slow roar was exhausting, to her mind and heart. She'd be able to sleep without fear of her car breaking down in the middle of the night while she and Aiden walked down lonely deserted roads.

Janet needed this win. It helped her believe, to dream of better days to come, days she hoped desperately would be happy ones.

She *was* going to make it.

*   *   *

Monday morning Teri came into the office. "I'm not married."

Janet put the box of receipts down. "I'm sorry?"

"I've never been married, to *anyone*. I don't know why she told you we were. She's staying at my house because she needed a place to stay after her divorce."

"Okay." She leaned against the table.

31

"I want to know what she said, because Kaitlyn claims she never said we were married, and you were exaggerating."

"Really?" Janet shook her head, "Well, let's see. She'd asked if I was interested in you. Said you've been together for over fifteen years…"

"We've been *friends* for over fifteen years."

"If I hurt you, I'd have to deal with her."

Teri clenched his jaw.

"I asked her about you dating Madison. Kaitlyn said the two of you were no longer together, and I quote, 'Besides, we have an open marriage.' End quote."

"An open marriage?"

"Mm-hmm."

His face and ears reddened. "Wow. She calls herself a friend. She knew I was interested in you. Why would she intentionally sabotage our chances?"

Janet shrugged, "Perhaps, she wants you for herself."

"Yeah, not going to happen."

She'd practically given up on having any kind of relationship again. The waiting for the end of the wretched drama her life had become was exhausting to her mind and spirit. She'd dreamed of happy days to come and wondered if there was happiness waiting for her, waiting on the other side of the darkness.

Her heart fluttered. Was there a chance for a relationship with Teri? She'd repressed her feelings for him for so long she wasn't sure what to do.

Janet moved forward with her life because she had to. She couldn't cower in a corner and surrender. She endured the niggling desire to give up and pushed forward for Aiden. She lived with a shred of hope; things would settle down and finally have smooth sailing amongst the winds of life.

Was she being naïve and blindly innocent?

She continued to plan a better life for herself and Aiden. Janet had given up believing she'd be lucky enough to share it with someone.

Why would Kaitlyn be so vindictive? What was her point?

She avoided people like Kaitlyn who were negative and manipulating. Her mom used to say, stay away from people who carried a dark cloud in their hearts. Get as far away from them as you can. *In time, they'll be so far away you'll no longer be able to hear their negativity.*

However, he and Kaitlyn were roommates. They'd be constantly circling each other. Janet would never trust the woman again, regardless of whether she dated Teri or not.

"Janet." Teri took her hand, "Now that you know the truth, will you go out to dinner with me?"

Was she walking into more drama?

She took a deep breath and plunged into the river of uncertainty. "Yes."

Chapter Five

Two Harbors, two-story, three bedroom, two bath, 1500 square feet, quarter of an acre…189,000

The seller accepted her offer of 180 and today it would be hers.

Janet's hands shook as she signed the paperwork for the mortgage to purchase the house. The realtor had been extremely patient with her. They'd probably looked at over twenty houses in the last few months. Janet knew exactly what she wanted and what she could afford.

The house was perfect. Aiden had seen it before he left for Texas, loved it, and had already picked out his room.

It was a fifteen-minute drive to work, and twenty to Aiden's school.

Easy peasy.

If only she could stop her stomach from churning with nerves.

She'd sent pictures to her parents. Her father was encouraging, telling her she was doing great. It was the perfect starter home.

Her mom's reaction was more reserved. *Oh, how quaint. You sure you don't want to keep looking, honey…*

Teri and George had both gone through the house with her. The electric box needed replacing, which Teri did.

George volunteered to fix the plumbing in the laundry room. The inspections came through with flying colors and the appraisal was right on target.

George and her dad talked on the phone as they did their walk-through before she put in the offer. George reassured her father it was a good investment.

Oy. She was buying a house all by herself.

X will be pissed.

A nervous giggle escaped, and she grinned. She was beginning to take pleasure in pissing him off. It really needed to stop. It didn't make life easier by baiting him.

It may not be the nice, big house she owned when she and X were married, but it was hers.

She did it. Not with anyone else's money, except her own and the bank's.

This was her little, cozy, *quaint* house.

Tonight was her first date with Teri, and a celebration on her closing.

A few hours later, he picked her up and they headed into town.

As they were leaving, Janet noticed her constant unwelcome companion had returned. The Charger was parked a few houses down from hers. An investigator X was paying to follow her drove it. It wasn't the first time, and it probably wouldn't be the last.

Ignore him and enjoy your time with Teri.

Teri pulled into the D's Pizza parking lot. Perfect! Now the question was; did he like it with pineapple?

"I hope you like pizza."

"I do."

Teri laughed. "I guess it's a good thing. We could go somewhere else."

"This is fine."

He held the chair for her and then sat across from her. Would you like some wine to celebrate your new house?

"Yes, a rosé or Zinfandel would be nice."

Teri sat back in his chair. "What do you like on your pizza?"

She put her hand on her chin. "Everything."

"Really? Even anchovies?"

"Yes, anchovies, pineapple, pretty much everything most people scrunch their noses at."

"I like anchovies. But, not so good with the pineapple on pizza though."

She leaned in and whispered, "That's okay. I won't hold it against you."

He lifted his draught. "Here's to you and your new house. To new beginnings."

She raised her wine glass and tapped his bottle. "To better tomorrows."

"What time do you want us there tomorrow?"

"I asked Jacob if he could be there at nine o'clock. Patti is scheduled for tours."

"I know you didn't ask me but, I can be there."

"I'm sure Jacob would appreciate the man muscles."

"The man muscles?"

Janet raised her arm and flexed. "Um-huh. Yours are bigger than mine."

He laughed. "I hope so. You look like you're barely pushing one hundred pounds."

She felt the heat flush her cheeks. Self-conscious, she looked down. "One twenty. I lost a lot of weight in the last few years."

"I didn't mean it as an insult. You look perfect to me."

Don't go there, Janet. Don't let your insecurities ruin your fun.

She took a bite of pizza, and closed her eyes. Delicious, fresh and hot.

Teri lifted the pizza and whispered to it, "How do you say hello to a pizza?"

Smiling, she asked, "I don't know. How?"

"Slice to meet you."

She groaned, and then chuckled.

"Hey, you don't think pizza jokes are *cheesy,* do you?"

"Never." Janet took the napkin off her lap and placed it on her plate.

He winked. "You just stole a pizza my heart."

"You sound like my dad. He loves dad jokes." Janet laughed and shook her head. "Between the three of you, I'll get my fill of dad jokes. Want to hear George's favorite?"

"Sure."

"How can you tell the punch line is a dad joke?"

"How?"

"It's ap*parent.*"

He laughed. "I'm going to have to remember that one."

"Of course you will."

"We'll keep you entertained for life. You want some dessert."

"No, thank you."

"How's Aiden?"

"I don't know. I've called a couple of times but there was no answer."

"I'm sure he's busy having a lot of fun."

Janet nodded, "Yes, they like to keep him busy when he's visiting them."

"What would you like to do next? Dancing? A walk in the park? There's a free band tonight."

She stood, and put on her sweater. "The park sounds like fun."

"Great."

As they were leaving, Janet noticed the Charger sitting a few spots from Teri's car. It pulled in when they arrived, and was still waiting for her to leave. Aiden dubbed him 'the watcher'. She was hoping it was her active imagination.

It wasn't. Janet wasn't surprised. The car followed, staying back far enough to be discrete as they headed to the park.

When they entered the park area, Janet turned around. The Charger pulled into a parking spot.

Not very covert buddy, or is it you don't care anymore?

Her lawyer told her to ignore him. It wasn't an easy thing to do. She wasn't doing anything wrong. She wasn't doing anything. This guy probably fell asleep on the job. She lived where she worked, and very rarely went out, except to pick up Aiden or go to the Grill with the museum group.

This is the first date she's been on in over a year.

She was boring. Her life was boring.

What was X trying to prove? Why was he having her followed again?

She gave her new address to the lawyer. The watcher will have some excitement now.

"Are you okay?"

"Yes, why?"

"You keep looking back."

"Oh, sorry." *Tell him.*

He put a blanket on the ground and popped open a couple of sodas.

Out of the corner of her eye, she saw 'the watcher' taking pictures. She took a deep breath and turned her back on the camera.

"I'm glad you finally agreed to go out with me."

"You had a cheering section."

"Oh?"

"Aiden, George, Patti, and Jacob all talked about how wonderful you were."

"Did they? Well, guess I better finish paying them what I owe then. They were quite expensive you know, tooting my horn for me."

She smiled. "I'm sure they were."

He tucked her chin and started to lean in.

She abruptly pulled away. The spark and the desire were tempting. *I want to kiss you. I want to touch you, caress every square inch of you.*

"I'm sorry. I thought…"

Janet shook her head. "It's not you."

"No kissing in public allowed?"

"No, not really, but it's not why."

Teri frowned.

"We have an audience."

He winked, "No one cares what we're doing."

She pointed toward the watcher. "There's a PI following us."

His mouth dropped. "What?"

"X randomly pays this guy to follow me. He was at D's, followed us here, and has been taking pictures."

"Why?"

"Probably still trying to prove I'm an unfit mother."

"Wow."

"Mm-hmm."

"I think you're a fantastic mother." Teri put his arm around her. "Let's give them something to talk about."

"In time." She put her head on his shoulder. *Why not?* Janet liked having his arms around her.

Chapter Six

X was livid. She couldn't understand why. He was getting married. What was his problem?

Sarcasm and spite dripped heavily with each word. "Ready to fail at another marriage?"

"We're dating, and marriage isn't on the table. Besides, what do *you* care?"

"Poor guy doesn't know what he's getting into. You're combative. You love to argue and you have a fierce right hook. I should probably warn him."

"Self-defense doesn't make me combative. I never started it."

"Yes, you did. You threatened to throw boiling water on me."

"You left speed, crossroads, within Aiden's reach. He could've eaten them and I would never have known what was wrong! He could've died."

"You're overreacting as usual. They were in my pocket where he couldn't have gotten them. You should've been a better housekeeper."

"I was picking up *your* pants off the floor in the family room."

"You've got a serious problem. I really should warn him about getting involved with you."

"I have. I told him if he ever hit me, he'd better knock me out. Because if I can get back up, my fists will be swinging."

"I remember your temper all too well."

"Well, perhaps you shouldn't have—"

"Your mouth is sharp and vindictive. It shut you up. Temporarily anyway."

"If you didn't want to be married to someone with a backbone, then you shouldn't have married me. Flanagans don't roll over and play dead. We come back fighting."

"I won't have those problems with Katie. She's agreeable."

"Yes, I'm sure she's quite accommodating and malleable."

Silence…

The grandfather clock in the hallway ticked away.

"Aiden will fly in at 8:00 a.m. on the 4th. I think it's Frontier. You need to pick him up. I'll be out of town."

Her hands were shaking, and her heart was racing. She wrote down the date and time. "Okay."

He hung up the phone.

Bait and switch.

Dingus. He knows exactly how to push my buttons. I fall for it every freaking time, too.

Teri came in and dropped off some paperwork for George. He kissed her on the cheek and mumbled, "Got to run."

They'd been inseparable since the first night.

He always brings a smile to her heart.

Janet was elated, falling in love again. She'd forgotten how great it was to just *talk*. He'd stay every night after work, leave for a few hours to sleep, and then return in the morning for work.

A few weeks later, they were laying on the bed watching a movie. A storm was rumbling in the distance.

"Let's go to the museum. I want to see it at night, when no one is around."

"Sure. It isn't any different at night than it is during the day."

He laughed. "You keep telling yourself that."

"Ghosts and specters walk the halls at all hours of the day."

He opened the car door for her. "I want to explore the west wing and the sanatorium."

"Well, aren't you the Indiana Jones of Locke Manor."

"Will it freak you out?"

Janet shook her head. "No, I lived there. I heard all the ghostly apparitions and their whispers."

Flashlights in hand, they entered the rear door near the west wing.

The two went on a journey through the darkened halls toward the old sanatorium. The brewing storm was getting closer, and the manor was preparing itself for the coming battle.

She soon learned he loved ghost stories and the paranormal. He was telling her about the ghost tours he'd done in the past.

Teri insisted he heard whispers and cries. "Can't you hear them? They're talking to us. There are secrets here. They dwell in the darkest corners hiding from the rasp of the winds. This place is haunted. I wonder if the watcher has caught any ghosts while taking pictures of you at the museum. I think I'll ask him next time I see his Charger."

"Please don't."

"Why not?"

"X will just fire him and hire someone else. This way, I know who it is. Sometimes, I think he intentionally lets me see he's watching. He knows he's wasting time, but won't turn down the pay."

"Good point." The wind howled. Lightning lit up the room. "I should've brought a camera. Next time."

"There are pictures, quite a few actually."

"What? I want to see."

Janet laughed, "Of course you do. Let's go back to the storage room, and I'll pull them out of the box. Some of them are pretty interesting. You can see body shapes, and then there are the typical spheres."

The two of them fell asleep on the couch in the office. The box of photographs with the apparitions and specters at their feet.

She woke stiff but happy. Janet smiled. She was falling hard. Teri was fantastic, and she knew they were a perfect fit.

To have a solid, loving relationship with him would be a chance of a lifetime. She'd thought she'd never find someone to love again.

She couldn't pass it up, couldn't screw it up.

Janet wanted to do everything she could to make this relationship work.

Her mother was right. *It's never too late to find love.*

Another tidbit of wisdom both parents always told her, we hold the key to happiness in our hands. Don't depend on anyone else to make you happy. It's on you to create your own happy.

She tended to block the bad and not let it ruin her day. Nevertheless, sometimes it was impossible. X was extremely difficult. He's still angry with her for leaving him.

Having Teri in her life made it easier. She felt bad getting him involved in all the unnecessary drama. She did warn him. He didn't care.

The air was filled with both good and bad dreams. Where did she hear that?

She started singing, *Mr. Bluebird's on my shoulder…*

He was her Bluebird of Happiness.

She felt hope again, and jumped out of bed ready for the day. When was the last time she felt optimistic? It'd been a constant drag herself out of bed, and prayers to make it through the day.

Being involved with Teri changed everything. Goodness, the first time he kissed her. Little butterfly kisses down her neck and chest. Her body shivered in anticipation.

She wanted to rip his clothes off right there and then.

Janet grinned, and the night before last when they'd been intimate, his eyes practically rolled back to the other side of his head.

Then, he returned the favor.

Yes, this was going to be a freaking awesome relationship. She'd thought it was too late to find love.

They'd had a lot more in common than she'd originally thought. He was fun and funny. He had an unlimited amount of puns he enjoyed dropping on the most unexpected times. He was a lot like her father in many ways. She smiled.

Aiden liked him, which was crucial.

X didn't. She grinned, even better.

She got up and started the coffee. Good thing she still had a change of clothes at the museum.

The phone rang while she popped muffins in the toaster oven.

"Mom."

"Good morning! You're up early. Goodness, it's good to hear your voice."

He whispered. "I snuck downstairs to call you. Are you mad at me because Dad made me come to Texas? I didn't want to go yet. I told him we had lots of stuff planned. Is that why you haven't called me? I don't want you to be mad at me."

Her heart tightened in pain. "Aiden, I'm not mad at you at all. I've called your phone almost every day." *Your father made you go?*

"They took my phone. Said I didn't need it and you'd call me on their phone."

"I don't have their number." *Your father wouldn't give it to me.*

"They said you did, and if you wanted to talk to me you'd call."

She grumbled, "Really?"

"I needed to know if you were mad at me." He sniffled. "I'm sorry, Mom."

Her heart broke to hear the pain in his voice. One more battle to fight. "You did nothing wrong. I'm sorry, Aiden. This isn't your fault. It's okay. This will be taken care of immediately. Are you having fun?"

Aiden proceeded to tell her all the things he'd been doing over the last few weeks.

After about fifteen minutes he whispered, "I have to go. They're awake."

She felt relief to hear his voice, and anger at X. Aiden shouldn't have to sneak so he could talk to his mother.

Janet took a deep breath. She will not let this ruin her day. She emailed the lawyer and put it in his lap. It's why she was paying him.

She broke a few eggs in the pan and started singing. *I see skies of blue...*

Teri leaned against the door. "You have a beautiful voice. Wow!"

Janet jumped. She hadn't heard him come in. "Sorry. Kind of you to say. The acoustics in the kitchen will make anyone sound good. I didn't know you were awake yet."

"Not the acoustics. You have an awesome voice. I'm surprised you didn't pursue a singing career."

She laughed.

"I'm serious."

"People just say it to be kind. Like some of those people on the talent show on television."

"Sometimes, but not this time. Who convinced you that you couldn't sing?"

Her eyes stayed down. Janet didn't say a word.

By the look on his face, Teri knew exactly who told her. "Never mind. I know who."

He poured coffee for the both of them. "You can sing for me anytime. I love your voice."

George walked in. "I agree."

"Et tu, Jorge?"

George grinned. "Yes. We could use a good, solid alto in our church concert choir. Try-outs are Monday night."

Teri asked, "You've heard her sing?"

"When she thinks no one's around, she tends to sing and hum when she's working."

Janet put a couple more eggs in the pan and eyed him. "Traitor."

Chapter Seven

Kaitlyn pinched Janet's arm. "You need to start eating. Perhaps when your son returns you'll start eating better."

Janet bit her tongue. She'd always been thin, and someone telling her to eat more was a sore spot. She didn't tell people they needed to lose weight. It was insulting.

Kaitlyn leaned against the counter. "You're too skinny. Teri likes women with meat on their bones."

"I only eat when I'm hungry. Unlike *some* people, I don't grab comfort foods. I can't eat when I'm upset."

Patti came out of the stall. "That's rude. How would you like it if she commented about your weight and thunder-thighs?"

Kaitlyn's face turned blood red and she snapped, "I wasn't talking to you."

Patti walked to the sink. "Why are you so spiteful?"

"I'm not. I just know what Teri likes."

Janet started to speak, but was cut off.

"How would you know? Have you done him?"

Kaitlyn's eyes twinkled, a satisfied smirk danced on her lips.

Janet sucked in a deep breath. Teri tolerated X, she can put up with Kaitlyn.

Patti responded, as she grabbed the door to leave, "He must've been drunk." Her hand mimicked a mic-drop before she left the bathroom.

They joined the guys at the table. They were talking about famous athletes and the women they've dated.

Janet asked, "How many people did you date before you married?"

Patti thought a few seconds, "I'm not married yet, but fourteen so far."

Janet counted ticking off names in her head. "Ha! Me, too."

Jacob was counting, ticking his fingers as he pulled up names in his head. "Twenty-two." He winked at Patti. "But I think that'll be it."

Teri said, "I'm only at eight."

Everyone looked at Kaitlyn.

She snorted, "Wow, and you called me rude. I can't believe you have the audacity to ask someone how many people they've f'd before they got married."

Janet was stunned. "I didn't. I asked how many people you dated. Not how many you have done. Two very different things. A person doesn't 'do' everyone they date, unless of course, you have airborne reckless leg syndrome."

Kaitlyn bared her teeth but didn't say anything.

Teri asked, "What's airborne reckless leg?"

Janet eyed him, wondering if he was joking.

Patti was more blatant. "You know, a woman who's free with her sexuality and indiscrete with her sexual adventures. Her reckless legs are always up in the air. No matter who, she does it, everywhere, with everyone she can."

Teri started coughing.

Kaitlyn's face turned beet red. "Well, Teri of all people knows I'm not like that. Besides, if a woman chooses to be a free spirit, it's her choice. Why is it okay for a man?"

Patti leaned forward. "No one said you were."

Kaitlyn scoffed, and flipped her hand dismissing Patti.

Patti snapped, "I don't respect a man who will do anyone and anything he can, no more than I respect a woman who does it."

Janet put her hand in the air. "Well. I—"

Kaitlyn sneered, "Keep thumping that Bible Patti. I suppose you want to crucify gays, and anyone else who doesn't go along with the norm."

"I don't care about any of those things. In my opinion, it's the disregard for self-respect and other people. Moderation is what matters, regardless of personal preferences."

"Backpedal much?"

Janet tried again. "She—"

"I'm not backpedaling in the least bit. What happens behind closed doors is none of my business. I *never* said what they did was wrong. All I did was tell Teri what airborne restless leg syndrome meant. You made the assumption."

"I didn't assume anything."

Patti sat back. "Bull."

She snorted, and looked at Teri. "I think I'm ready to go home now."

Teri looked at the group. "Yeah, good idea."

He got up, kissed Janet on the cheek, and whispered, "I'll meet you at the house."

Janet nodded.

After they left, Jacob, Patti, and Janet looked at each other. The silence was heavy.

Finally, Jacob said, "Wow."

Both Patti and Janet nodded.

Patti asked Jacob, "Do you know if Teri's had sex with Kaitlyn?"

Jacob turned his head toward the bar. "Why do you want to know?"

"Because, she pretty much came out and said she did."

His knee started bouncing and he hesitated. "Ahhh."

Patti put her hand up. "Never mind."

Janet grabbed her sweater. "It doesn't matter to me. I think I'll call it a night as well. See you in the morning."

Patti sat forward. The tension was visible in her upraised shoulders. "Are you upset with me?"

"Absolutely not."

"You sure?"

She hugged Patti. "Yes, I'm sure."

Patti took Jacob's hand. "Okay, we'll see you tomorrow. Be careful driving!"

On the drive home, Janet wondered why Kaitlyn was being so cruel. It couldn't be jealousy. Why did she feel threatened? What was her problem?

She was too old for this high school drama.

Teri's car was in the driveway and she pulled in next to it. It made her smile to know he was home waiting on her.

She kicking her shoes off and looked at Teri.

The first thing out of his mouth was an explanation, "She wanted it to be kept a secret."

"I don't care. It would've been nice to know so she couldn't blind-side me though."

"I'm sorry. You're right. I should've said something. I never thought it would come up."

"Why would she want to keep it a secret?"

"Didn't want any of our friends to know." He handed her a glass of wine, and they sat in the lanai.

"Why would they care?"

Teri shrugged. "I don't know. It was a one-time thing."

"A one-night stand?"

He cringed. "No, it was just the once."

Okay. She chuckled. "I don't care. Good thing Patti didn't know. It would've been interesting to see her reaction."

"Why doesn't Patti like her?"

"Because she's a trouble-maker."

"No." He frowned and shook his head.

"Sorry, but she told Patti I wanted to marry you for your money. Supposedly, I had three mortgages, and needed your paycheck so I wouldn't lose my house and car."

His voice was sharp. "What?"

"Yup. Patti told her if I wanted a rich man I'd go back to the Hamptons."

"Why didn't you say something?" Teri clenched his jaw. "It's not what real friends do. What is her problem?"

"I don't know, and I'm sorry, but I don't want her in my life."

Teri pulled on his ear.

Janet put both hands out. "You can be friends with her all you want. Go to lunch, meet for dinner, I don't care. However, I don't want to have anything to do with someone who carries so much unhappiness with her. X brings more than enough drama to my life as it is. I'm too old for this crap."

"I'm sorry."

"It isn't your fault."

"I need to find out what her problem is."

"She didn't say anything to you on the way home?"

He grunted. "She asked if you were going to move in."

"Move in? Why? I just bought *this* house." She made a puffing noise with her lips. "If anything, you'd move in here."

Crickets...

Janet's heart raced. The more she thought about it, the more she liked the idea. She felt happy and secure when she came home and saw his car in the driveway. She knew she was loved, and he was there waiting for her — waiting to love her.

X's voice mocked her...*you'll never make it without me. You're too much of a princess.*

Someday, you'll be a real wife.

You're useless.

Why don't you get a real job?

You need to learn how to cook.

You're never going to make it...

Her eyes began to fill. A lone tear dripped from the outer corner of her eye. Why did it still hurt so much? She wanted Teri. Could she make him happy? Would she be successful this time? Or, crash and burn?

He took her hand. "I would like that. Although, I've never lived with someone. Well, except roommates."

She kissed his cheek. "It's not any different except you have to share three-quarters of the bed with me."

Teri chuckled. "I love you."

"I love you, too. When Aiden comes on Tuesday, let's talk to him about it. Once we get the 'Aiden stamp of approval' we're good to go."

Chapter Eight

Janet turned off Airport Road. Aiden hugged her long and hard when she'd picked him up at the gate. All the way to the car, he'd talked non-stop about the last few days in Texas, and the airplane flight. He'd been thrilled with the window seat.

All she heard was the hum of the engine as they headed to their new home.

"You're so quiet."

He shrugged.

"I can't wait for you to see what I've done to the new house. I left your bedroom untouched. I want to go with you to pick out the paint and new furniture."

"Sure."

"Are you okay? Is something bothering you?"

He shook his head.

Aiden shifted uncomfortably in his seat, and stared out the window.

"Teri is looking forward to seeing you. He should be arriving at the new house right before we do."

Aiden smiled. "I'm glad you're still seeing him."

"I made corned beef and cabbage."

"Grandma made it last night for me."

She frowned. "Oh, okay."

He bit his lip.

What was bothering him? "I can freeze it and we can have it another night. What would you like for dinner?"

"No, it's okay. We can eat it. Grandma said I needed to eat what you served, even if you couldn't cook."

Janet's eye started twitching. "Can't cook?" *Did X tell his mother I couldn't cook?*

Aiden stared out the window. "Mom, don't get upset. It's okay."

No, it's not.

There was no need for her to defend herself. Aiden knew her. He lived with her half the time. Eventually, he'd see the truth. She needed to take the high road, and not lower herself to mimic their negative behavior. She had to continue to be herself and Aiden would soon understand their deceit and schemes to discredit her. The fear of manipulation went beyond X to his parents, and lord knows whom else he's lied to about her.

Janet thought she'd purged the fear and guilt. All she'd done was bury it, and it still haunted her. She had an even greater motivation; to prove X wrong.

The lies cut back across time and seared her heart. It stunned her. It shouldn't have, but it did. The poison of lies opened ancient wounds beyond which the remedies of time couldn't erase. She knew the truth should have healed her. To hear it coming from Aiden's lips crushed her spirit.

Silence hung heavily in the air for the rest of the ride home.

Teri was standing in the doorway, waiting to greet Aiden.

Aiden looked happy for a second and then frowned. "Is he living here now?"

"No—"

"Good. Grandma said only whores live with men before they're married."

"What?" *Is wrong with her?* Janet sucked in a deep breath. "Grandma's calling your father's girlfriend a whore?"

Aiden shook his head, confusion danced across his face. "No, she meant you."

He walked past Teri with barely an acknowledgment.

Teri took Aiden's suitcase from her. "What happened?"

Janet's eyes watered. "I don't know! He was excited to be coming home when I spoke to him yesterday afternoon."

Aiden stayed quiet through all of dinner. Teri and Janet attempted several times to get him to talk about his trip to Texas, what he'd like to do with the room, and the upcoming school year. They received shrugs and cold shoulders.

He ate three helpings of the corned beef and cabbage. He put his plate aside. "May I leave the table?"

"Yes, put your plate in the sink. Do you want help unpacking?"

Aiden stood and answered from the kitchen. His voice was sharp and abrupt. "No."

Janet responded, "No, thank you."

Aiden snapped and stomped up the back stairs. "No, thank you!"

A few hours later, Teri headed home. Neither one of them could figure out what was going on with Aiden. Janet checked in on Aiden before she went to bed. Burrowed comfortably under the sheets, all she could see were his eyes and nose.

Dawn and its faint rays of sunlight awoke Janet as they crept across the sides of the walls of her bedroom. After her morning ablutions, she knocked on Aiden's door to wake him. There was no response. He'd always been a heavy sleeper and she didn't think anything of it. Janet headed downstairs and started the coffee.

She called up the steps, "Aiden, come on. It's time to go. I have to get to work."

When he didn't answer, she went up to his room.

He wasn't there. She looked about the room. His backpack was gone, and the suitcase was practically empty.

She ran through the house searching for him and calling his name. She ran outside and looked in the yard.

Terror filled her heart. Aiden was gone.

She couldn't dial 911 fast enough.

On the phone, she explained X was out of town, the boy wouldn't have gone there. She requested they drive by there anyway.

Next, she called Teri, and then George. Teri called off work and arrived must faster than the speed limits allowed. He'd arrived before the police.

Walking along the roads, he searched the woods near her house while she paced in the living room. The police were a blessing. They'd kept her calm, while they took photographs of his room and a picture of him from the mantle.

She had to make the dreaded phone call to X. Needless to say, he was furious. The last thing he said was, "Not even home for twenty-four hours and he can't get away from you fast enough. He's hiding somewhere. I'll be home in a few days. Call me when you find him."

She stared at the phone when he hung up. *Wow.*

The next day, she went to work for a couple of hours. She'd felt useless at home, and being at the museum wasn't helping. The next day, Janet tried to go to work again. Patti complained about a mouse in the west wing, and Janet came in to lay a trap. Teri stayed at the house, just in case Aiden showed up.

He can't get away from you fast enough.

She heard a noise in the room next to the back stairwell. She walked into the room and opened the window. The shutter was banging against the outer wall. The haunted museum was fulfilling all the clichés.

She headed down to the kitchen.

It was a great beautiful manor. For Janet, the whispers and creaks were common, for anyone else it'd be a night of terror. Yes, she'd had a night of terror, but it wasn't from the specters haunting the estate. Her small boy disappeared into the night.

Was he in danger? Would the danger cost him his life?

Was Aiden just hiding as X claimed?

It was a new day at Cedar Ridge Hills. The lake beyond shivered in the clear morning air. As she sat in the kitchen, heart thundering in her chest, terror mounted. Aiden hadn't been found yet. Far from the comfort of the warmth of the kitchen, her son may be in danger.

Dread of what could be happening to her baby gripped her. It was a fear so terrifying it stunned her mind and numbed her heart.

Janet had gotten no sleep. She'd been running on pure adrenaline. She couldn't count how many times she'd pushed through the wall of exhaustion. She could hear his voice.

Mom.

Aiden, where are you?

Mom, help me.

Janet snapped her head up. She'd dozed. Was she dreaming?

She heard Aiden's tearful voice. *Mom.*

Janet looked around. Where was it coming from?

"Mom." Aiden's voice was weak.

She walked slowly over to the wall, near the rear passageway the help used from the past. She pushed on the latch, and it swung partially open. Something was jamming it.

"Ow, stop. That hurts!"

"Aiden!"

She picked him up and carried him to the chair. "Oh my God. What happened?"

"I came here because I didn't want to be at the new house. I want to live here. I don't want to live in the ghetto." He sobbed. "I was hungry so I came down the servant's stairway. I couldn't see and fell down the stairs. I think I broke my leg."

Janet was already calling an ambulance and the police.

"Where does it hurt?"

He showed her his swollen ankle. She felt around but couldn't really feel anything. At least, if it was broken it didn't break through his skin.

She put an ice pack on it. "Hold this and stay here."

"Don't go."

"I'm going to get you a blanket."

"No. I'm hungry."

"Okay. Peanut butter and jelly?"

He nodded. "I broke my phone when I fell."

She handed him the sandwich. "Aiden, why did you run away?"

"I want to live here."

"But, Sweetie, you helped me find it. You loved the house when we first looked at it."

"It's in the *ghetto*."

"Excuse me?"

"Don't be mad, Mom. I know it's all you can afford."

"We don't judge people by where they live or how much money they make. It's how they behave, and whether they're honest and hard-working. *Not* where or how they live nor what they look like."

"Daddy said it was."

"It *isn't* the ghetto. Locke Bay doesn't even have one."

"Daddy said I didn't have to live there."

She gritted her teeth. Another scar added to her tongue. Oh, what she would truly love to say. She restrained herself. "You do have to live with me, until you're old enough to live on your own. Daddy is misinformed. Let me show you something."

Janet grabbed the tablet on the table. She typed in ghetto, clicked on images, and handed it to him.

"People really live in those places? I thought it was only in the movies."

She shrugged. "I'm not rich, Aiden. I make a decent, honest wage. I work hard for you, and myself. Is it as much as your dad or your grandparents? No, not even close. We don't need all those luxuries to be happy. I have a good job I love, a nice new car, and a good home. We have Teri, and we have each other. It's all the matters."

Aiden put his arms out for a hug. "I'm sorry, mom."

Teri ran in and joined in on the hugs, just as they could hear the sirens. Janet shook her head. Breaking speed limits again, he beat the ambulance and the police.

Aiden was crying, and mumbling, "I'm sorry."

Later that night, after her lengthy shouting match with X, Teri and Janet sat down with Aiden.

Teri handed Aiden a bowl of ice cream. "We have a question for you."

He took a mouthful and said, "Okay."

"Your mother and I discussed moving in together, but if you don't like the idea…we won't."

"I think it would be awesome, but I don't understand. Why does Grandma and Daddy think it's wrong for you but okay for Daddy?"

Janet grunted. "Good question." *How do I dip my toes into that poisonous pond?*

Aiden waited, expecting more.

"Some people feel it's okay for them to do certain things, but not acceptable for others."

Aiden tilted his head.

Janet tapped her fingers on her leg. Different scenarios ran through her head. *Got it.* "Okay, how about this? You ask for cookies and I tell you no, it's too close to dinnertime. Yet, I go ahead and eat a couple while I'm making dinner."

"That's not fair. If you can have one I should be able to have one."

"Right. That's how it should be…with most things."

"Why most things?"

"I can have a glass of wine, but you can't because you're too young. Things like that."

"Oh, okay."

Teri asked, "So, we're good, Buddy? I can move in here with the two of you?"

Aiden stood and walked over to Teri. "Yes, I think it'd be great."

Chapter Nine

Two years later

The horse whinnied and stood patiently waiting for the toddler to quit squirming.

Janet watched as Aiden taught his baby sister, Emma, how to control Boots. Aiden was a great big brother. He was growing so fast, becoming a fantastic young man.

A little late in life, Emma had been a pleasant surprise, but worth every ache and scare.

Teri was ecstatic. Their parents couldn't have been more pleased.

She was terrified. What if she screwed up again?

Three months after she married X, she wanted to leave him. Her mother talked her out of it, convincing her it was just a typical, newlywed argument and would be resolved over time.

Over two years with Teri and it was pure bliss. Teri was wonderful. He'd kept all his promises, and then some.

He did the dishes and helped with the laundry. He didn't care it was 'women's work'. He did what needed to be done, with no hesitation.

He got up in the middle of the night to take care of Emma, when she'd been exhausted and slept through the crying. He changed her diaper, gave her baths, and got on the floor and played with her.

When Aiden caught the flu, he helped take care of him. They did father and son things together. Teri attended all of his games and matches. He never hesitated to support Aiden in anything he wanted to do.

He even helped him with schoolwork.

He and Aiden would come to the museum and do work together, fix things that needed to be repaired. Teri would be patient, explaining to him how and why it needed to be done a certain way.

The adoration went both ways.

Aiden was constantly talking about Teri. It thrilled Janet. Her two men got along swimmingly.

She looked up when Emma squealed, "Mommy, I'm a cowgirl!"

She waved as they rode across the pasture.

Cedar Ridge Hills Museum finally hired a new curator, and it looked like Thalia Jefferies would stick around for a while. Janet loved every haunted moment she was there. She hoped Thalia would too.

She leaned on the fence post. With a serene, satisfied smile, she took a deep breath, closed her eyes and faced the sun. What a beautiful day.

She'd always said when she grew up she'd want a horse grazing in the back pasture, and a pool table in the family room. Now she had both.

Guess she could officially call herself a grownup now.

Today, she and Teri celebrate their second anniversary. Even though there were a few rough patches, Janet knew it would last a lifetime.

What a huge difference between X and Teri.

X would stir up trouble and Teri would stand up to him. No hesitation. He was a beautiful force of love on her and Aiden's side. It felt good to know someone had her back.

He was all she hoped for in a relationship. Janet made a wish, and he came true.

Teri always encouraged her. He made her feel appreciated, even during those times when all they did was argue.

They didn't have the mansion, or anything fancy, but they had a pot of gold in their hearts no one could take from them. It didn't do any good to have the luxuries in life if you couldn't share them with the ones you loved.

She'd come a long way from the "comfortable" lifestyle of her childhood. Walking away from X was the hardest and best thing she could ever have done.

What a story it's been.

If only she could tell it, without having a lawsuit chasing after her. Sad, but too many of the abused never speak up. They're shamed into silence.

Someday, the victim will no longer be at fault.

There were times when she knew she'd been out of her realm, bit off more than she could chew. How cliché. Unfortunately, it was too true.

She'd made every attempt to let go of her anger, resentment, and insecurities. It was hard. For so many years when she looked in the mirror, she saw an unrecognizable broken, shattered face staring back at her.

She'd been so broken. Many times, she'd wondered how she'd gotten herself into the mess she'd been in, and why she didn't get out sooner.

She scoffed. Fully aware it was her stubbornness and determination to make her first marriage work. She didn't want to give up. Marriage was supposed to be forever, through thick and thin, better or worse, 'til *death do you part*'.

The only problem was, death may have been by someone's hand.

Those doubts still haunted her, but as much as they chased her, Janet wouldn't give up or give in. They weren't all on X. The sad truth boiled down to it being on her. They were her decisions, and she lived with the repercussions and was accountable for her part in it all.

Many of the emotional cracks were still there. Perhaps, some may never be repaired.

However, she moved on. She would keep the happiness she was given, her second chance for love, and prove to herself life could be wonderful.

Why hadn't she gotten out and walked away sooner than she did?

Her whole personality changed from being bright-eyed, and thrilled with life, to a malevolent, angry person.

Perhaps it's why she tolerated Kaitlyn. She saw the unhappiness in her.

Janet was back to being herself again. Happy, comfortable, and ready for any challenge life would throw at her.

Marriage wasn't easy, even when you're with a fantastic person. It took commitment, and a passionate desire to succeed. If there was no abuse of any kind, physical, emotional, mental, it could work out.

Otherwise, don't bother.

Such a negative attitude.

When Janet took the leap of faith into a life with Teri, she'd begun to let go. She began to forgive herself, and X. Even though he continued to be combative, she refused to let it ruin her life.

If she hadn't given up, she would've never met Teri or given him a chance.

Forgiveness wasn't about the other person who hurt you...it was about moving on.

It lifted a huge weight off her soul.

She made a promise to herself years ago she wouldn't let life's tragedies keep her down.

She chuckled to herself. Sure, because the hell she'd been through didn't take away the rose-colored glasses and punch her in the face with reality.

She got herself a new pair.

Janet, *you will not* become a bitter old lady with a perpetual frown.

She wouldn't allow it. There was always a promise of tomorrow. She'd made it. She's finally found her Bluebird of Happiness.

Her second chance for love.

Mr. Bluebird's on my shoulder...

Dear Reader,

I hope you enjoyed *Skies of Blue*. It was originally a story in the charity #TeamPink4Teri Late to Love Box Set stories.

"Faith, hope, and charity, but the greatest of these is charity."

Turn the page for a preview of The House on Cedar Ridge.

Thank you!

Have a good moments day,
Pam

Stories that stir within us the unquenchable hope for a better tomorrow.

Time traveling adventurer, award-winning multi-genre author, Pamela Ackerson was born and raised in Newport, RI where history is a way of life. She lives on the Space Coast of Florida where everyone is encouraged to reach for the stars! When it's time to run away, she's a hop, skip, and jump from Disney World and fun-filled imagination and fantasy. With over 70 books under her fingertips, she writes time travel, westerns, Native American, historical fiction, nonfiction, WW2, inspirational, self-help marketing and advertising, personal and travel journals, and children's preschool/first reader books.

PamelaAckerson.net

Pamela Ackerson

@PamAckerson
Facebook.com/pam.ackerson.7
Email: PamAckerson@adcmagazine.com
Amazon.com/Books-Pamela-Ackerson

Sneak Peek

The House on Cedar Ridge

Chapter One

Her journey began there, on a cold, windy day, with an ominous warning of what was to come. It brought her to a strange, dark place near the edge of the great Lake Superior. The manor, called Cedar Ridge Hills, rose high atop the hill.

She grabbed the keys in the box next to the door. At this late hour, no one would greet her. She was to let herself in and set up her quarters in the western wing on the second floor past the office area.

Thalia Jefferies hoped her journey would open the doors of life, and bind her past with her future. The ornate, French doors unsealed an unfamiliar world with people she never met, people who were only shadows in her imagination, but would soon fill her tomorrows.

It was a dark and frightening place on the crest of a lonely hill. The ghosts of yesterday cautioned her to leave, but Thalia had arrived, and there was no turning back.

The fear of darkness and the unknown was only for the young.

She walked through the desolate corridors of the mysterious, dusky manor. Thalia could hear the brooding calls of the dead trembling in its walls, and singed her unexpressed fears. It was her home now and the outside world fell away into distant shadows.

There were homes with warm, welcoming families in Locke Bay, people with hopes and dreams. Yet, she couldn't feel anything but the dark night as it pressed its gloom on her. It crushed against the windows whispering to her, telling her to escape while she could.

It was a fitful sleep but, at least, the night was over. It was a night touched with a fear Thalia had never known before. The gray light of early morning brought no relief from the heaviness that inhabited the house.

Thalia was enjoying a cup of coffee when a well-dressed man entered the kitchen area.

"Good morning." He put his hand out to shake hers.

She stood to greet him. "Good morning. Thalia Jefferies, you must be George Greene?"

"That I am. Local expert, docent of a little bit of this and that, and *way* too many stories. Sit, please. Finish your breakfast. I'll pour myself a cup and join you."

She watched the elderly man as he heated a cinnamon roll and poured coffee into a cup. He sat across from her. "It's good to see you're still here. You lasted much longer than the last curator we hired."

"Oh?"

"He didn't make it past midnight."

Thalia laughed. "Well, it is a bit scary up here at the top of the hill. It's an odd and lonely place. I enjoyed the grounds at sunrise this morning. All I could see was the great hulk of Cedar Ridge towering above the mist, a sleeping monster on its crest."

"I like that, good thing you'll be helping with the tours. In your email, you said you wanted to do some deep, ancestral searching. I know a lot of local history, and would be happy to help."

"Thank you. I'm really curious about—"

A group of people entered and introductions were made. The museum would open soon. It was reassuring to see the nametags on the employees; she was never very good at remembering names. Faces, yes. Names? No.

Thalia hoped and believed the answers she was looking for might be here—for her father, if not for her own personal curiosity. At the end of each day, she'd wait in the darkness and search the dust of hidden years, surrounded by ghosts of the past and shake away the fears of the present.

Thalia pulled folders out of the filing cabinets, she'd have a lot of work to catch up on and understand. Normally, the director would train her, but Cedar Ridge didn't seem to have one.

She wondered what happened.

Thalia started reading notes from the early 1900s when the Locke family moved to another home away from the cliffs. It'd become a sanatorium for about fifty years before they closed the doors and an order to demolish was aborted. The people of Locke Bay, and the historical society saved the beautiful manor.

Whoever put notes to paper described the dead past with a colorful flourish as they recorded the history of the family. She could picture them as they drifted through the corridors of Locke Manor, now known as Cedar Ridge.

The pages of stories settled like dust in its corners. They worried a legacy would be destroyed, yet spurred by hope, they fought to keep the manor in place.

Her search continued as life itself continued. Not only for her but also for everyone else in this strange corner of the world. There was so much history here. Would she find Albert, her long-lost uncle? Would she be able to release her father from the haunted memories of two young children in search of family?

Locke Manor was a sanatorium, a foundling home, hospital, and a place for those whose devils prowled the hidden hollows of fear. People who lived with their own trepidations and their own hopes.

It was of a forgotten time as foundlings and the infirm made their home on the crest of the hill. The great house echoed with their pain.

It was a lonely and frightening place. For Thalia, it was a place of hope. It was a home where the winds of the past would bring the answers to the future.

Patti, one of the tour guides, walked into her office and leaned against the desk. "You know, you've been here for almost a month. Why don't you come into town with us? We're going to a restaurant on the water. It's beautiful in the evening. Something I think you'd like to see."

Thalia smiled. "I think I'd like that. Thank you. Sometimes the mysteries of this place make me feel like it's reached out and touched me and everyone within its walls."

"The longer you stay, the more it will become a part of you. It'll feel like it's closing in on you."

"I think that's called cabin fever."

"Yes, well, you can get it real easy here at Cedar Ridge."

"I'll keep that in mind."

"Meet us at six? At the Superior Oyster Bar and Grill."

Thalia waved as Patti left the office. "Sounds good. Thanks."

She looked around her office. Yes, it'd be easy to get lost in the past. It could become a prison, not only for her but also for others, and anyone driven by fear of the future.

Cedar Ridge sat for over one hundred years in brooding isolation on the crest of its hill. Thalia looked at the shadows of the manor in her rearview mirror.

She was afraid, to leave, and to stay. The great house on the hill carried the dusty smell of fear. The secrets of its past lived within its darkened rooms. They moved through the paneled rooms and corridors seeping down from the walls.

It touched the heart of everyone who entered.

∞   ∞   ∞

The group sat around the table and gotten quiet when she'd arrived. It immediately put Thalia on guard.

Jacob, the groundskeeper for the museum, pulled out the chair next to him. "Come on. We were just talking about you."

"We want to know why you've stayed," Patti said, before handing her the menu.

"We sure do," Janet piped in. "And, how you can stay at the museum with all its ghosts and legends."

"It's just a house. I don't believe in ghosts."

"You will." Jacob smiled at the waitress who'd approached the table. "Know what you want?"

"Yes."

Patti grabbed some clam cakes. "Aren't you scared?"

Thalia shook her head. "Not really. I mean sometimes it's a bit spooky."

Janet harrumphed, "that's putting it mildly."

Patti flipped her hand outward. "I've stayed there at night. It was terrifying. The night wind battered the hill with the force of a thousand demons. I felt so alone as if there was no town beyond the crest, only the waves, the wind, and the terrible loneliness of fear."

Jacob laughed. "Can you tell she wants to be an author?"

"It's true. The house is surrounded by tension and sometimes it grows so tight, it chokes you."

Thalia was curious. "Why do you work there?"

Patti pulled her hair up. "The daytime is fine. The nights come alive with ghosts of the past. You wouldn't get me near that place at night."

Thalia looked at Janet. "What about you. Do you believe in ghosts?"

Janet chuckled nervously and pointed to her empty wine glass when the waitress came by. "Don't forget I lived there for well over a year."

Jacob took a drink from his mug. "You should find a place in town. Get out of that house before it swallows you."

"Definitely," Patti agreed vehemently. She took a bite of her chocolate cake. "Get out now, while you can."

∞ ∞ ∞

On the drive back, Thalia couldn't help but hear the ring of truth cast at her feet. The great, dark house on the crest of the hill was alive with ghosts of a past she never knew. Ghosts that drew tight fingers around the present.

Thalia wasn't about to let them sway her determination and would continue her search. There were answers in the dead past at Cedar Ridge. She knew there was a connection between her father and his early life. She would learn what happened to his brother, and where he went. The answers had to be there, somewhere.

She would find them.

Searching the dusty corridors on the third floor, the wind howled against the glass windows. Dark threads of the past tied her to the great house on top of the hill. Her search was endless as the corridors wound about. Each room echoed dark voices of fear. Thalia listened to their murmurs and trembled as she approached the door where the strange voices called.

She looked about the tattered room with its musty, torn furniture, and broken lamps.

There was an odd stillness about the room. Dark voices of fear scolded her in the upper floors of the great house that was now her home.

She opened a chest. It had clothing from a bygone time. Nothing to note, nothing to give her clues to the hidden hollows of the past. She approached a large table, strewn with assorted items, books, and papers.

Grabbing a photo album, she carefully opened it. Dust billowed upward and she sneezed.

She picked up an elaborately decorated fan. She traced the edge. It appeared to be ivory. She opened it and fanned herself. Smiling, she slipped her finger through the ring on the end.

The door slammed behind her. She jumped and dropped her flashlight and the photo album she was inspecting. Moving toward the door, she grasped the knob. She was shut in, locked somehow. She banged on the door, knowing it was useless. She was alone. All had gone home for the night.

A brewing storm buffeted the walls. There was no sound in the house, nothing but the echo of thunder and the whine of the rising wind. The emptiness was alive with an encumbering fear. It was built on a simple, terrifying fact. Thalia was alone.

She tried the door again to no avail. She sat on the floor in dismay. The room was hot and musty. She cooled herself with the ivory, scrimshaw fan until sleep crept into her tired body.

Thalia awakened, stiff and sore. The sun streaked muted rays through the covered windows. She stood and leaned against a bureau, waiting for the dizziness to pass.

Thalia inspected the door. The hinge pins were removable. If she could find something to use to remove them, that'd be a blessing.

Her eyes scanned the room in the sunlight. It looked different, less threatening and spooky. She shook her head. No need to go there. The howling wind was bad enough; she didn't need her imagination making things worse.

The early morning mist rose from Lake Superior at the foot of the hill. Angry spirits out of the dim past seemed to pound against the door, demanding admission.

Her heart raced. Something wasn't quite right.

She put the fan in her pocket and grabbed the flashlight.

Before she attempted to take the door off the hinges, she reached for the handle.

The door swung open.

Here in the hidden crevices of Cedar Ridge was a moment of quiet, even the wind subsided, and the threat of a storm was past.

However, there were other storms to come.

She grabbed the photo album and quickly left the dark crevices of the third floor. Relieved the night was done.

"Who are you and what are you doing here?" the voice of an unfamiliar woman demanded.

Thalia slowly turned. "Who are you and how did you get inside the museum?"

The woman had her hair pulled back so tight her face looked pinched and angry. She was in odd garb, a long, dark gray skirt and blouse with a functional apron covering it.

"Your attire is indecent, showing off your legs like that. There are men here, you know."

Thalia looked down at her dress. It was a conservative sheath dress with a matching jacket. Quite reasonable for business attire. It was a bit dusty from the room, but that shouldn't cause the kind of reaction she was getting from this woman.

Was this one of the apparitions?

"You need to change your clothing immediately. Then, I'll take you to Dr. Huey."

"Dr. Huey?"

"Yes, the man who runs this sanatorium."

"Sanatorium?" Thalia stood unmoving, unsure of what she was to do and what was expected.

"Girly, is there something wrong with you? Stop repeating what I'm saying to you with a question."

The great house sat quietly on its crest and the events unfolding were but a dream, a nightmarish vision from a shattering night confined in a dusty room. It couldn't be real yet, it was almost like a vague memory of a forgotten dream.

Thalia stopped following the commanding woman. "I'm not moving one more step until you tell me who you are and how you got here."

The woman leaned in closer to her face. "You don't look like an idiot."

She grabbed Thalia's arm. The woman was surprisingly strong, but Thalia was definitely stronger. She twisted the woman's arm, releasing the grip. "Who are you?"

"My name is Catherine, and I'm the headmistress of the school."

"School?"

"Yes. Where did you think you were?"

This was no dream. The woman in front of her was real.

Thalia felt lightheaded. She could feel the heat flush her face and a buzzing in her ears.

"Girl, are you well?" The woman grabbed her arm. "Come with me."

Chapter Two

The woman brought her into a room. "Stay here. I'll be right back."

Within moments, the woman returned and handed her some clothing. "Here. This looks your size. Put them on and while you're doing that, you can tell me how you got into this section of the facility without anyone seeing you."

Thalia put the photograph book and fan onto the bed. "I work here. I'm the curator."

"We have no *curator*. What's your name, girl?"

"Thalia. Thalia Jefferies."

"You came from the closed section of the house, didn't you?"

"What?"

The woman handed her a cap. "How'd you get in there?" She waved her hand frantically. "Never mind. I don't want to know. Too many apparitions and devilish stories. If you're going to be here, you're going to work. Can you teach?"

"Yes...but—"

"Good. We need a teacher. This will be your room."

"But, I don't think I'll be staying." *If I can figure out how to leave here.*

"No freeloaders. You work while you're here. Come with me."

Thalia followed the woman to the lower level and entered an office area. The paneled rooms and corridors were familiar, but she was a stranger walking through the passageways of the gloomy, old manor. She was even more determined to uncover the secrets hidden inside its walls. Her first night in the dusty attic brought her here to this unknown world, a realm filled with mysteries.

Here she stood at Cedar Ridge, in front of her office. Yet, it was not.

The gentleman at the desk looked up from his ledger. "Good morning, Miss Catherine."

"Good morning, Mr. Walker. Is Dr. Huey available? I'd like to introduce him to Miss Jefferies."

"He's with Mr. Locke. One moment."

Miss Catherine whispered, "I don't know why I'm putting myself on the line for you; I have a notion to…"

"You may go in."

They entered her office but in this strange dream, the hidden echoes of the past were moving closer and closer. The woman who brought her here was a mystery as well.

Thalia was more certain than ever that somehow the unanswered questions of her father's past entwined with the hidden secrets of Cedar Ridge itself.

Here she stood, in the present and in the past. A mystery echoed through all of Locke Bay, reaching out to others as well.

Miss Catherine spoke to the doctor. Thalia noted the furnishings and the two men in her office. Both appeared to be about the same age.

The doctor wore typical physician's garb.

The gentleman standing near the window was not. His attire wasn't from her time. He stood regal in his striped pants and tailcoat. He held his top hat, and a cane rested upon his arm.

Thalia always did like a man in formal attire. She found it sexy and compelling. The aura of regal class. She knew this was typical for this man.

They stood staring at each other, neither one wanting to be the first to look away. His eyes were piercing in an unusually pleasing way.

She wanted to walk over to him and introduce herself. Where was she? Perhaps, she should ask *when*.

"Miss Jefferies?"

Thalia blinked. "Yes ma'am?"

"If you could take your eyes away from Mr. Locke for a moment, the doctor would like to ask you a few questions."

The heat of embarrassment flushed her cheeks. Mr. Locke appeared to have the same reaction. His face was a vibrant shade of red.

"Dr. Horace Huey." Catherine put her hand out. "Miss Thalia Jefferies."

"A pleasure, I'm sure. This gentleman is Marcus Locke."

Thalia nodded a greeting.

Dr. Huey asked. "Have you worked in a sanatorium before Miss Jefferies?"

"No, sir."

"Do you have a degree in higher learning?"

"Yes, sir. I attended St. Mary's College in Notre Dame, Indiana."

Why didn't she pay more attention to the history of the school?

"That's a good school. When did you finish your courses?"

"In 2018."

His eyes widened. "Excuse me?"

All three people in the room stared at her dumbfounded. Her chest tightened. What was she supposed to say?

"Pardon me. I'm a bit nervous and reversed my numbers. I meant eighteen to twenty months ago."

It appeared to appease the doctor for the time being. Mr. Locke, not so much. He eyed her warily.

Dr. Huey asked, "Do you have any experience in the medical field?"

"I took a few first responder, EMT courses."

"EMT?"

"Emergency medical technician."

"That will be quite helpful. Our facility holds a wing for hospital patients, a small section for foundlings, and the western wing is the sanatorium. You will be teaching the foundlings, and assisting in the hospital ward, and at the sanatorium when needed. Since you have medical experience, we'll start you at thirty a month, including room and board."

"Thirty?" Thalia couldn't stop the distress in her voice. "*Dollars?*"

"Yes, we're being quite generous. Most newly engaged teachers receive sixteen a month. But because you have medical experience, we can offer you more."

She needed to wake up from this hallucination, this nightmare. Thirty dollars a month? They can't be serious. She was making that per hour at Cedar Ridge Hills!

He flipped his hand. "Miss Catherine can give you the tour of the facilities."

Mr. Locke spoke up. He was silent throughout the entire interview. "I'd like to join you, if I may?"

Miss Catherine restrained a grin and turned a querying brow to Thalia. "Of course."

Miss Catherine started in the hospital section, introducing her to the doctors and nurses. She wrote Thalia's name down and scheduled her for two evenings a week. She continued talking about the history of Locke Manor, how it'd become a hospital and sanatorium.

Mr. Marcus Locke walked beside them, quietly listening to his family history. Miss Catherine explained the Locke family owned the facility. He was the last of the family who lived in the area, excluding an aunt who was admitted to the hospital as a permanent patient.

He built another, smaller home for himself at the bottom of the hill on the Locke property, and created the hospital and sanatorium. In time, there was a need for a foundling section, and it was then the children started arriving.

"I understand your compassion, Mr. Locke, but a foundling home is a huge undertaking, especially considering the hospital and sanatorium."

"It was most distressing to see the homeless children on the orphan trains."

Thalia reassured him. "Surely they were found good homes."

Marcus' eyes were distant in memory. "Some did, and many were thrown to the wolves. I'd arrive in Duluth on business and see the waifs. There was a vacant look in their eyes. Cold, like the black, dark sky hovering before a storm. It reflected their haunted and shadowed lives.

"They watched unblinking and impassive to the terrors that stalked beneath their feet. They were lost, indifferent to life, and death. It reminded me of a final gasp of breath. Perhaps they saw from the cold corners of the alleyways, the fate that lurked beyond, and waited for the last, silent struggle for life."

"I never realized it was that bad."

Miss Catherine touched her arm. "None of us did. Marcus has a huge heart. He wanted to protect the homeless orphaned children. The reformers have a good plan. Some take advantage of the system. The idea was to get them away from the squalor and poverty, not to use them as child laborers."

"And so, you opened the foundling home, to educate them and help them find good, loving homes. How do you get the children?"

Catherine answered, "They're usually the children who weren't adopted, or perhaps were troublesome and unwanted. We have a couple of gentlemen we work with who bring the children to us. Every once in a while, they bring a couple of children from Duluth and other areas."

His warm smile rested upon Miss Catherine several times during her guided tour. "Sometimes."

When they stopped at the sanatorium section, Miss Catherine pulled out her keys and they entered the area. "We'll just schedule you for one evening a week for now, until we see how you fare."

Thalia nodded, looked about the area and the long corridor of rooms.

"Most of them stay locked away in their rooms. However, some are allowed into the public area for socializing."

Mr. Locke appeared uncomfortable. His breathing had increased and his eyes darted about the room. Miss Catherine took his arm. "Come Marcus. We have no need to stay."

His reaction had a story behind it. More secrets and ghosts of the past added to the legends of the old house on the crest of the hill. Hidden echoes moved closer from within the walls and crevices, and Thalia was desperate for answers.

"How long have you been here, Miss Catherine?"

Marcus held the door open for the ladies, and Miss Catherine turned to lock them away from the residents of the sanatorium section.

"About twenty years."

"Twenty years! I didn't realize the hospital was around that long."

Marcus answered, "It hasn't. Miss Catherine was my tutor and mentor. She practically raised me. When I no longer needed her services as a governess, and no longer needed a house this size, she stayed on to work at the hospital, and then, to tutor the foundlings."

"I probably haven't left here in ten years."

Thalia searched her eyes, curious. "Ten years?"

"There was no need. Everything I need is here. I'll walk the grounds; go down to the beach area of the lake. It's all on the Locke property. Although, there are times when Marcus insists I join him for dinner at the local inn."

"Otherwise, you'd pine away waiting for the ships to return, staring out the window or near the edge of the cliffs." Marcus leaned toward Thalia. "*You* have no cause to do that, Miss Jefferies. We could enjoy a meal or dessert at one of the fine restaurants in Locke Bay. A stroll in the evening on the Locke grounds is very pleasant as well. The view of the lake can take your breath away."

"It would be my pleasure, Mr. Locke."

"Marcus, please. No need for formality here. May I call you Thalia?"

"I would like that."

The two women watched the young, handsome man as he walked away. He belonged here, yet didn't. There was a haunting within the walls, and they seemed to follow him.

Catherine turned to her. "Beware of getting attached to Marcus. He pines for his betrothed."

"He's engaged?"

"They believe Winifred was lost at sea. She was supposed to return from England almost a year ago. He is still in mourning."

"How horrible."

"She wanted to travel before she settled down to a provincial life. Winifred was an adventurous sort, and felt her future at Locke Bay was at the edge of provincial damnation."

"But it's so beautiful here!"

Catherine grunted and handed her a set of keys. "Welcome to the end of the world."

Made in the USA
Columbia, SC
30 March 2023

14229199R00050